Written by
Andrew Melrose and Judy Waite
Illustrated by Garry Davies

For St Luke's Junior and Infant Schools, Brighton

Bramble Hill

How would you feel if your school's football team had made it to the Cup Final, and your big brother was the star player? It would be great, wouldn't it? But then, what if you were going to move to a new school? And what if that new school just happened to be the other team in the Cup Final? What if your brother was playing for his old school against his new school? Might there be just one or two problems?

Leafield

Chapter 1
Just a Game?

Alice stood on the touchline and booted the ball to her cousin, Billy. The ball skidded wide. Billy went panting after it.

"Come on, you two! I'm falling asleep here!" Her brother, Tim, leant against the goalpost and pretended to snore.

Alice pulled a face at him. "All right, show off! We know you're Bramble Hill's star goalie, but we are helping you practise for your Cup Final against Leafield Juniors tomorrow."

"Helping me?" Tim laughed. "I'm going to forget what a football looks like if you don't shoot it this way soon!"

Alice stuck her tongue out. Then she
laughed, too. She wasn't really cross
with him. Tim was a brilliant goalkeeper,
and she was proud of him.

Billy came panting back with the ball.
"You know I probably shouldn't be seen
playing with you," he said.

"Why not?" Alice asked, as she tackled Billy – well, sort of tackled him. There was so much space between Billy and the ball, you could have parked a row of buses there.

"Well, I go to Leafield Juniors, don't I? That means you two are supposed to be my rivals," said Billy.

"We won't be rivals once we move house though, will we?" said Alice, as she dribbled the ball round him. "We'll be on the same side then."

"That'll be great." Billy smiled at her.

Alice smiled back. Billy often looked worried, but when he smiled it was like the sun coming out. She kicked the ball to him again. Billy tried to kick it back but he skidded and slipped in the mud.

As Alice helped him up, she heard footsteps behind her. She looked round to see Shane Parker from Leafield Juniors strolling towards them.

"So what's this then, Silly Billy?" sneered Shane. "Are you passing our team's secrets to the enemy?"

"Shane the Shark, what's he doing here?" Billy whispered to Alice. He looked worried as he wiped his muddy hands on his jacket.

Alice looked worried too. Shane Parker was the striker for Leafield.

"I know what you mean," she whispered back. "Shane's had it in for Tim ever since he got picked to train with the Football School of Excellence. He goes there one afternoon each week. Shane's really jealous of him."

"Hi!" shouted Tim. He wasn't worried about Shane being there. "Are you going to join in?"

Shane growled, "I wouldn't waste my energy running around with you lot."

"You're right," said Alice. "You're going to need it all for tomorrow!"

Shane glared at Alice. "Not if your brother knows what's good for him," he said.

Tim looked puzzled. "What do you mean?"

"I mean, you'd be a bit of an idiot if you helped your team win, wouldn't you?" Shane went on.

"In what way?" Tim asked.

Shane began flicking the ball. "Well, how's it going to look if you're the one who makes Leafield lose the cup? Do you reckon we'll give you a hero's welcome when you join our school next term?"

Tim looked Shane straight in the eye. "You don't scare me."

"I might not scare you," Shane bounced the ball hard onto the ground, "but what about your kid sister?"

"What about her?" Tim was frowning now.

"You might be able to look out for yourself, but you won't be able to look out for her all the time." Shane turned to Billy. "Tell them I'm right, Silly Billy," he said.

Billy didn't answer.

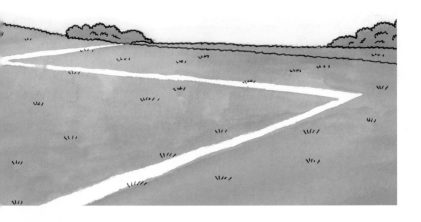

"Hey, I'm talking to you, Silly Billy!" Shane bounced the ball again. "Perhaps you should let these new kids know what life's like at Leafield for those who don't fit in."

Suddenly, Shane kicked the ball past Tim. Tim wasn't ready for it. He wasn't even watching. He was worrying about Alice.

"GOAL!" laughed Shane, running and snatching the ball back out of the net. Then he booted the ball to the other end of the pitch and walked off. Tim, Alice and Billy watched him go.

"Ignore him, Tim," said Alice. "He wants to put you off so you play badly tomorrow."

Tim put his arm round Alice's shoulder. "Don't worry. I won't let a bully like him spoil things."

Billy looked worried. "You don't know him like I do," he said. "Maybe you *should* be worried. You don't know what he does to kids he doesn't like."

But neither Alice nor Tim were listening to him. They were already walking away across the park.

Chapter 2
Chicken?

"It's great to be playing in the final," said Spiky. He was the right winger for Bramble Hill. He smiled at Alice as their bus drove through the gates at Leafield Juniors. "Bramble Hill have never made it this far before."

"Leafield have won for the last three years," added Big Bruce Tomlinson. "But with Tim in goal, we stand a really good chance this year."

Alice smiled back at them both. She knew how much the cup meant to Tim. Even though he was leaving Bramble Hill to go to Leafield Juniors, she knew Tim really wanted to do well.

Tim wasn't on the bus. He'd spent the afternoon at the Football School of Excellence and was cycling to Leafield after training.

"OK, everyone, get your boots on," said Mr Johnson, the Bramble Hill teacher who coached the team.

Everyone scrambled off. Alice watched them walk to the changing rooms. Then she looked round for Tim. There was no sign of him.

"Where's the star goalie then?"

Alice swung round to find Shane standing there. "He's coming on his bike," she said.

"It would be a shame if he'd fallen off," grinned Shane.

"It's the only way you lot would have a chance of winning," Alice snapped.

The grin dropped from Shane's face. "Or perhaps he's just too chicken to play."

"Why would he be?" Alice began to walk away from him.

"Like I said yesterday, by the end of this game, either Bramble Hill will hate him for letting goals in, or we'll hate him for keeping them out," said Shane.

"He still wouldn't back out," Alice replied.

Just then, Alice spotted Robbie
Robson wearing Tim's goalie jersey.
It was much too big for him. It looked
more like a dress. Robbie looked upset.
He called out to Alice, "Mr Johnson said
we couldn't wait for Tim any longer.
I'll do my best for the team until Tim
gets here."

Alice smiled at Robbie, but she felt upset too. Robbie would try his best, but he wasn't Tim.

Shane leaned towards Alice and whispered, "Chicken!" Then bending his legs and tucking his hands up into his armpits, he shouted, "Cluck, cluck, cluck!" before he strutted away onto the pitch.

Alice felt someone touch her shoulder.

"Don't take any notice of him." Billy was standing there. He looked hot and flustered.

"He doesn't bother me," Alice said. "I'm just worried about Tim."

Billy looked down and scratched his hands nervously. "Maybe Tim really *has* decided to stay away."

"He wouldn't," Alice told him. "He wouldn't let everyone down like that."

"But, it might be more sensible. I mean, Shane's right ..." Billy scratched his hand again. " ... life would be rough for you here next term if Bramble Hill win today."

Alice shrugged. "Well I don't care, and neither would Tim."

Billy looked worried. "I'd better go and start cheering for Leafield."

He walked off to watch the match from the other side of the pitch. Alice went to join the other Bramble Hill supporters.

Bramble Hill kicked off, but it was a bad start. Straight away, Leafield got the ball off them and rushed up the pitch.

A minute later, Shane had the ball in front of the goal. Poor Robbie had no chance. When Shane kicked the ball over his head, all Robbie could do was watch it dropping into the back of the net.

"GOAL!" shouted the Leafield team.

"Never mind, lads," Mr Johnson said to the Bramble Hill team. "There's a long way to go."

Shane ran past Alice, shouting, "Cluck, cluck!"

After the kick off, Bramble Hill did their best. They had practised in rain and snow for this match. This final was all they'd cared about.

A Leafield player dribbled the ball and then passed it to Shane. Shane raced past Spiky and turned towards the goal. Big Bruce Tomlinson moved closer, but Shane kicked the ball through his legs.

Robbie Robson was onto it in a flash. Just as Shane drew back his foot to shoot, Robbie kicked the ball away and sent it for a corner.

"Yes!" shouted Alice, forgetting for a moment that Tim was missing.

But she cheered too soon. Leafield had two big centre backs and they had come up for the corner. Shane took it quickly. Robbie tried to get to the ball, but it was no use, Leafield's biggest centre back reached it first.

For the second time in the game, Robbie was picking the ball out of the back of the net. For the third time that day, Shane was making chicken noises at Alice. She tried to ignore him, but she couldn't ignore the worried faces of the Bramble Hill team.

As Bruce Tomlinson walked back to the touchline, he shouted to Alice, "How could Tim let us down, today of all days?"

Alice was about to shout back that she was sure Tim would be here at any minute – but before she had a chance, the referee was blowing his whistle. It was half time and there was still no sign of Tim.

Chapter 3
All Square?

As the game started again, Alice was even more fed up. Tim still hadn't turned up. She stood a little way off from the other Bramble Hill supporters. She didn't want to hear them grumbling.

Alice hated to admit it, but Shane was a good player. Bramble Hill were still trying though. Robbie pulled off a brilliant save that even Tim would have been proud of. Then Robbie booted the ball upfield. Jimmy Jones, the Bramble Hill winger, pounced on it and kicked the ball into the back of the net.

"GOAL!" shouted Alice, jumping up and down with excitement.

33

Shane was furious. He picked the ball out of the net and kicked it at Alice.

Alice missed it and the ball disappeared into some bushes by the caretaker's shed. Alice marched off in search of it. She found the ball half hidden in a clump of nettles. She grabbed it and threw it back towards Shane, giving a yelp of pain as the nettles stung her hand. Then she noticed something else hidden in the nettles. It was Tim's bike.

Alice was puzzled. How did it get there? "Tim?" she called, looking all around.

Suddenly, there was a shout from inside the caretaker's shed. "Alice? Is that you?"

Alice forgot about the stinging nettle rash that was spreading across her hand. She knew that voice. "Tim! What are you doing in there?" She ran towards the shed.

"I came in here to see if there was somewhere I could put my bike," Tim shouted back. "Someone pushed me from behind and slammed the door. Quick! Get me out!"

"I bet it was Shane. I told you he was scared of you being in goal!" Alice was angry. "Do you want me to call Mr Johnson?"

"No, not yet," said Tim. "There'll be a big fuss, and they'll probably stop the match. Just look for the key to this door."

"OK." Alice tried to keep calm. She had to think what Shane might have done with the key. There was a chance he'd have thrown it somewhere nearby. Then she saw something shining in the nettles. "I've found it!" she shouted.

Alice undid the lock. Tim ran out of the shed. "What's the score?"

"Two-one to Leafield!"

"Then there's no time to lose!"

Tim raced towards the pitch. Alice followed him. A huge cheer went up from the Bramble Hill side.

"Ref!" shouted Mr Johnson. "We're bringing on a substitute!" He waved to Robbie Robson who was already running off the pitch.

Tim ran towards his goal. "Right lads – let's show them what Bramble Hill can do!" he shouted.

Now there was no stopping them. They played brilliantly. Leafield still managed a few shots on goal, but nothing could get past Tim. Finally, in the last minute, Bramble Hill got a corner. Tim knew it was their last chance to equalise. He raced up the pitch.

"Where's he going?" screamed Alice. "He's left the goal wide open!"

"He has no choice," said Mr Johnson. "It's the last kick of the match. It's our only chance."

"Spiky!" shouted Tim.

Spiky looked up and spotted Tim running towards the Leafield goal. He kicked the ball from the corner and Tim headed it first time. It went straight into the back of the net.

The Bramble Hill team all jumped on Tim to celebrate. Alice leapt into the air and screamed, "Tim's scored!"

Leafield kicked off again, but a second later the referee blew the whistle for full time.

Shane stomped off the pitch. "It'll have to be a replay," he said angrily.

"But at least Tim will be there from the beginning," said Alice. "As long as you don't lock him in the caretaker's shed again." She scratched the nettle rash on her hand.

"Eh?" Shane looked puzzled.

"You know what I mean," said Alice. "You pretended Tim was too chicken to turn up for the match. But really you stopped him from getting there."

"You're crazy," Shane growled.

Alice scratched her nettle sting again. "Who else would have done it?"

Billy walked over. He looked worried. "So it's a replay next week?" he said.

"But Shane won't be playing," replied Alice, "not after I tell Mr Johnson about him cheating."

Shane was shaking his head, still looking puzzled. Billy suddenly blushed brighter than a beetroot. He scratched his hand, too.

"Wait a minute," said Alice. "What's happened to your hand?"

Billy shrugged. "It's just nettle rash. I did it before the match."

Shane frowned. "The only nettles in this school are by the caretaker's shed. I know because I'm always having to fish the ball out of them."

Alice looked Billy straight in the eye, just as Tim came over to join them. "It was you, Billy, wasn't it?" she said in amazement. "You locked Tim in the shed."

Billy was redder than ever. "I …" Then he nodded, staring down at his feet. "I'm sorry."

"I didn't want Shane to bully you," he
said. "I was scared about Bramble Hill
winning. You're my cousins, and I really
like you. I didn't want Shane to give you
a hard time later."

"Oh, Billy, that was a terrible thing to
do," Alice said.

Billy looked really upset. Suddenly,
Alice wasn't angry with him anymore.
She just felt sorry for him.

She turned back to Shane and said, "It may not have been you who locked Tim in the shed, but in a way it was your fault. Billy was trying to protect us from you."

Shane shrugged and turned to Tim. "Wait till the replay – then we'll see who's the better player."

Tim looked at Shane. "I don't care how good a footballer you are. I reckon bullying is the worst sort of foul play."

Shane shrugged again. He looked at Billy, then looked back at Tim. "OK," he said grumpily. "I'll leave him alone. It was only meant to be a bit of a laugh anyway."

"I don't think Billy found it very funny," said Tim. "But we'll forget it for now – just as long as there's no more trouble between now and the next game."

Shane looked as if he was feeling sorry. As Alice watched him, she thought he seemed smaller suddenly – more like a tadpole than a shark.

Shane shrugged, and then he grunted, "OK." Then he nodded to Billy before walking away.

"I don't think there will be any more problems from Shane," said Alice. "Whether we win or lose, I think he'll be fair to all of us from now on."

Alice looked at Billy. He was standing there with that big smile on his face – the one that looked like the sun was coming out. Alice smiled back at him. She was looking forward to the replay already.